Wizard Dog

This book is the property of

*Haberdashers' Aske's
School for Girls*

Infant Library Trolley

Removed

D0260137

To Toby Lisle *RL*

To Marieke *HS*

First published in Great Britain in 2009
by Andersen Press Limited
20 Vauxhall Bridge Road
London SW1V 2SA

www.andersenpress.co.uk
www.rebeccalisle.com
www.hannahshawillustrator.co.uk

All rights reserved. No part of this publication may be reproduced,
stored in a retrieval system or transmitted in any form, or by any means,
electronic, mechanical, photocopying, recording or otherwise,
without the written permission of the publisher.

The rights of Rebecca Lisle and Hannah Shaw to be identified
as the author and illustrator of this work have been asserted by them
in accordance with the Copyright, Designs and Patents Act, 1988.

Text © Rebecca Lisle, 2009
Illustration © Hannah Shaw, 2009

British Library Cataloguing in Publication Data available.

ISBN 978 184 270 890 3

Printed and bound in Great Britain by Bookmarque Ltd., Croydon, Surrey

Wizard Dög

By Rebecca Lisle
Illustrated by Hannah Shaw

LIBRARY
Haberdashers' Aske's School for Girls
Elstree
WD63BT

ANDERSEN PRESS • LONDON

LIBRARY
Haberdashers' Aske's School for Girls
Elstree
WD6 3BT

Chapter 1

Wizardless

This is a story about a ghost, a royal nitwit, three wacky wizards . . .

. . . and a very handsome dog.

A very handsome *pedigree* dog with a large brain.

Yes, you guessed it, *me*, Pong, the Royal Wizard's helper.

Well, I *used* to be his helper, but Wizard Wazp has disappeared, so now I help myself.

I live at the top of the tallest tower of the Royal Palace, in the Spell Chamber. I sleep on the Wizard's bed, on a heap of cast-off cloaks, ancient stockings and forgotten charms.

I do not miss Wizard Wazp. He was bossy and mean. So I was enjoying life until the King – what a twit! – ordered the rose garden to be dug up to make an ornamental lake for his daughter Princess Petunia. She and Prince Trevor are away on their honeymoon right now but they both love swimming.

This new lake turned out to be A BIG MISTAKE.

I was watching the gardeners from my window as they dug up the roses, thinking how the old Queen, who'd loved the roses, would be turning in her grave, when there was a knock at the door. A little pageboy stuck his head in.

'Message for you, Wizard!' he yelled.

The King is such a noodle: he hasn't noticed there *is* no real wizard any more!

Up until this moment I'd been playing at being the Royal Wizard without actually *being* the Royal Wizard. I could sort of work some spells and charms and there were some things I could do with the magic wand.

But you see, I actually did want to be the Royal Wizard. Somehow I had to get the King to give me that title. But how?

First, I thought, I had to look the part. I had tossed out several of Wizard Wazp's older gowns for recycling on Wednesday, but there were still three wardrobes packed with his clothes so I picked out a flattering blue gown for myself. A slight reduction in size, a few stitches, a button or two and it was perfect. Wizard Wazp had hundreds of pointed hats: I chose a green one and cut that down to fit. I looked, well, *wizard*!

At 5 pm I presented myself to the King.

Chapter 2

Tricked

The Royal Adviser Ambrose Smugpantz sat beside the King. The Adviser is a very round-bellied man with black hair so straight it looks like it's been ironed. His nose looks like a hippo sat on it.

I do not like Ambrose Smugpantz. He has advised the King to ban dogs from the Royal Garden. He even wants a law passed saying all dogs should wear a collar. He's against any barking after nine o'clock. Smugpantz is my Number One Enemy.

I turned away from the Adviser and smiled at the King.

'Your Majesty!' I bowed. And wagged my tail which is fluffy like an expensive ostrich feather fan.

'Who are you?' said the King. He peered at me. He didn't seem impressed with my tail. 'Do you know, I don't mean to be rude or anything, but you look like a dog!'

'I am a dog. The Wizard's dog, remember? Pong.'

'Is there a pong?' He sniffed. 'Can't smell a thing. Maybe I didn't change my socks this morning?'

'No, no, Pong is my name. P.O.N.G. It's short for Prince Oswald Nikon the Great. I'm a pedigree Shippo Pom-Pom from Japan.'

'Huh. Foreign, eh? Still, funny name for a dog. Even funnier name for a wizard – unless he did, you know, pong. Then it would hardly be polite. Where is the wizard? I need a wizard.'

'Our old Wizard Wazp's gone,' I reminded him. 'One of his tricks misfired. But don't worry, I was his assistant and everything *he* knew, I know.' Not absolutely true, but worth a go.

'You have only to ask and I shall do whatever wizardy things you wish.'

'Rubbish,' Smugpantz said. 'You can't. You're a blooming dog.'

'You think so too, do you, Adviser?' the King asked, nodding and grinning, happy to be right about something for once.

'A dog, but not an ordinary dog,' I said.

'Dogs chew bones, chase cats and bark – not wizardly at all. A dog cannot be a wizard,' said the Adviser. He rubbed his snub nose and leered horribly at me. 'Let me demonstrate the dog's small brain to you, Your Majesty. Listen carefully, little doggie, what is the brown stuff on tree trunks?'

'Bark!' I said.

Ambrose Smugpantz clapped his hands. 'Proves my point exactly!' he said as he turned to the King. 'It's a dumb dog.'

'You tricked me! Try me again,' I growled. 'Ask me another question.'

'What's that thing on the top of a house called?'

'A chimney?' I suggested.

'No.'

'Thatch?'

'No, it's red and made of tiles.' The Adviser raised his black eyebrows and sort of poohpoohed under his breath, as if I were stupid.

There was no way out. 'Roof? A roof?' I said.

'Yes! He's doing it again! Don't go on and on woofing and barking at us!' The Adviser chuckled. 'We know you're just a dog.'

'Not *just* a dog,' I said. My hackles twitched between my shoulders.

'And I *need* a magician,' said the King.

'Why do you need a magician?' I asked.

'It's nothing to do with you!' Smugpantz snapped.

'It's not a secret,' the King said, sadly. 'I'm being haunted.'

Chapter 3

A Ghost

'A *ghost?*' I said. The hair on the tips of my ears tingled. My tail quivered. 'Wow!'

'Wow!' repeated the Adviser. 'He's barking again.' The Adviser shook his head. 'Tut, tut. Dogs!'

'Yes, a ghost,' said the King. 'It screams and moans and cries like a baby. It wakes me every night. I'm scared witless!'

I think the King was witless before the ghost appeared, but I didn't say so. 'Maybe I could suggest—' I began.

But the horrid Adviser interrupted me. 'If we do not have a Royal Wizard in the Palace, we

certainly need one. We will post a proclamation
at the Palace gate immediately.'

'But you've got me!' I said.

Nobody took any notice.

'I like proclamations!
Jolly good,' said the
King. 'Here, doggie!'
He threw me a scrap
of biscuit.

Catch!

But I turned away in disgust and the biscuit crumbled across the floor. I hate to see food go to waste, but I am not a performing circus animal and refuse to demean myself.

'Pah, look! He can't even catch!' the Adviser said. 'What a dumb dog!'

Grrrr! Less of the *dumb*! I scampered up the 146 stairs to the Spell Chamber growling all the way. You'll see, Smugpantz! I thought. I shall catch the ghost and then you'll *have* to make me Royal Wizard.

I knew what the Adviser was trying to do with all his horrid comments. He wanted to make me ashamed of being a dog, as if a dog is not as good as a human. He wanted to weaken my confidence so I'll give up trying to be the wizard, but he won't win.

Hah, I'd rather be a dog than a human like Smugpantz any day! Who'd want his big flat feet or silly hair and squidgey nose when they could have my four dainty paws, silky fur and long wet black snout?

I will not give up!

I needed a spell. To catch a ghost I needed a *spell*. The trouble is, Wizard Wazp's spell books are very difficult. He used to have an alphabetical set which was easy, just go to G for ghosts. But one day I was using them as a makeshift staircase to reach the top shelf when F, G and H shot out through the window.

The other spell book is called TESCO. TESCO stands for *Thorne's Encyclopedia of Spells, Charms & Oddities*. I don't know who Thorne was, but he must have been a twisted, difficult character because that's how his spell book is.

When I tried to open the TESCO I couldn't. There was a message on the cover that said: Closed for Bank Holiday.

Great!

Chapter 4

A Squirrel and the Proclamation

The Advisor had written out the proclamation requesting a new wizard and nailed it up at the Palace gates.

NEW WIZARD WANTED

MUST BE WIZARD
AT WORKING MAGIC

WONDERFUL AT WIPING OUT WITCHES

GREAT AT GETTING
GHOSTS & GHOULS

NO DOGS NEED APPLY

NEW WIZARD WANTED

MUST BE WIZARD' AT WORKING
:MAGIC:
WONDERFUL AT WIPING OUT
WITCHES'
GREAT AT GETTING GHOSTS
AND GHOULS
NO DOGS NEED APPLY.

NO DOGS? Well, thanks, Hippo Nose, I thought. I love you too!

I did not want any passing wizards to see that notice and apply for the job. I had to remove it as quickly as possible. But the proclamation was too high for me to reach. I needed a ladder . . .

23

A sudden movement caught my eye. An aroma of acorns, crushed leaves and flea-bitten fur swept through the air near my quivering nostrils.

My brain burned. It popped and fizzed.

I dashed at the squirrel. It ran. I sprinted after it. It zigzagged this way and that with its

bushy tail streaming behind it like a cloud of exhaust fumes. The trees were too far to run to so it raced to the only safe place there was – the railings. As it scampered up the railings and over the gate, it scrabbled across the paper. The paper proclamation tore – instantly ripped to unreadable shreds.

I sat and watched. Wagged my tail and smirked. End of Wizard Competition, I thought.

The squirrel perched itself on the top of the gate and bared its teeth at me, jabbering rudely. Luckily I don't speak squirrel. When it had got tired of that, I calmly ate three or four bits of proclamation that had drifted to the grass because it seemed advisable to remove the evidence, and went on my way.

Job well done.

Hopefully I'd destroyed the notice before any wizards saw it. Now I just had to prove how clever I was and catch the Palace ghost. Since I had no magic or spells, I would have to use cunning and brain power, and luckily, being of such fine breeding, I have oodles of both!

I wandered back into the Royal Garden, pondering on what to do next. And while I pondered, I peed.

I peed on the trunk of an oak tree.

I peed on a bench leg.

I peed on the grass.

And still managed to pee out a few more drops against a flowerpot before I was done.

I felt so frisky I chased two fat speckled hens off the lawn and gave them a good barking at.

But my high spirits were soon dashed. There was bad news back at the Palace. Somehow, despite my efforts, *three* wizards had applied for the job.

Chapter 5

The Three Wizards

The King and the Adviser interviewed the three new wizards in the blue room at tea-time. I hid beneath the table where I could see and hear everything.

The first wizard was very, very OLD. He had long white hair and thin legs and arms like bits of bent wire. He hobbled up to the King and spoke in a trembling voice.

'Your Majesty.'

He tried to bow, overbalanced and bumped his long nose on the King's knee. 'Whoopsidaisy. Sorry, sorry. So so really very sorry,' he croaked. 'Do you mind if I sit down?

I'm feeling a trifle dizzy.'

'Name?' Smugpantz snapped.

'Wizard, er. Wizard um. Wizard whatwasit?' the wizard muttered into his grizzled white beard. 'Bah! Seem to be having one of those, what's it called? What are those moments called when you can't remember anything?

A something or other . . . I don't know. I can't remember my own name.'

'I have a photographic memory. I remember everything!' Smugpantz said smugly. 'And I know I've seen you before. Your name is Wizard Whitelock.'

'Whitelock? Ah! That rings a bell!' The old wizard chuckled. '*Dong, ding!* Yes, heard that name before. I think you're right, Adviser, I am Wizard Whitelock. Have we met?'

'Take a seat over there,' Smugpantz said, 'if you can stagger that far, you crumbling old thing . . . Next!'

The second wizard looked familiar . . . He was round and short with coal black hair that stuck straight off his head as if it had been ironed. An overweight hippo (or possibly two) appeared to have sat on his nose.

'This is my brother,' Smugpantz said, beaming. 'He is the finest wizard in the land.'

'Wonderful,' the King said. 'Do take a seat. How are you at catching ghosts?'

'The best,' the wizard said. 'Actually, I'm the best at everything.'

'Just like his brother,' Smugpantz said, puffing up like a bullfrog.

The King looked at them both. 'Which brother is that, then?'

'*This* brother,' said the wizard. 'That one there.'

'Which one?' The King gazed around vaguely.

'Oh, never mind!' the Adviser said. 'Sit over there, Botty.'

'Botty?' The King looked confused. I *was* confused.

'My mistake,' said Smugpantz, going red. 'Botty's what we call him in the family.'

'What an odd name.' The King rubbed his head thoughtfully. 'How did he get a name like Botty?'

'It really isn't important,' the Adviser said, glowing scarlet.

'Do tell!' said the King. 'I insist. And I can insist,' he said, adjusting his crown, 'because I am the King.'

Smugpantz gazed at the floor. 'His nose,' he muttered. The Adviser didn't look smug for once. 'When I was little I thought his nose was like a bottom. So I called him Botty.'

The King screamed with laughter. In my hiding place behind the tablecloth, I chuckled too.

Botty Smugpantz glowered at his brother. 'Idiot!' he hissed.

The third wizard was young with masses of curly hair. His wizard clothes were old, much washed and oddly familiar. His very brown eyes sparkled, as did his very white teeth.

I have always been a little suspicious of neat white teeth. Mine are pointed and yellow.

'Watcha!' he said. 'Heard you were looking for a Whizz!' He smiled widely at the King and then at the Adviser.

'A *wizard*!' Adviser Smugpantz said crossly.

'Yeah, one of those too! I'm Winston the Whizz.' He sat down by the table. 'Nice place this,' said Winston. 'Nice nosh.' With a wink, he passed me down a cream bun.

Never mind the teeth, I thought, at least this wizard's human. 'Thanks!'

'Do you have your qualifications to show us, Mr Winston?' asked the Adviser.

'Certainly do!' Winston said, handing over a sheaf of aged-looking documents. 'I'm much older than I look, you know. I mean what's the point of knowing tricks and wizardy spells if you don't use them to iron out a few wrinkles and neaten one's knobbly knees, eh?'

I could see that the documents were fakes, made to look ancient. And he wasn't old either, he didn't smell old. Old people smell like a bone that's been chewed, licked and gnawed until all the flavour's gone. Winston *smelled* young and fruity – he still had lashings of marrow in his skeleton!

I sniffed again: there was an interesting, *familiar* smell on his gown too. What was that?

'Just three magicians?' the King asked. 'Is that all?'

'It seems to be. It's very odd . . .' Adviser

Smugpantz glared at the door as if he expected more to come in. 'Oh, well. You know why you are here, wizards. We want a new Royal Wizard to replace Wizard Wazp. Your first mission, should you choose to accept it, is to capture, ensnare, disable or somehow do away with the ghost which is haunting the King.'

'Groovy!' said the young wizard. 'I'm a good ghost hunter.'

'I'll win. I'm the best at everything,' Botty Smugpantz said.

'ZZZZzzzzzzz,' Wizard Whitelock snored.

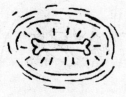

Chapter 6

The Wizards Make Plans

I needed to find out what the three wizards' ghost-catching plans were, so I slinked round the Palace to spy on them.

I soon sniffed out the two Smugpantz brothers in the library reading up on the history of the Royal Palace. They didn't even notice me as I came in behind the Adviser.

'The ghost might be Sir Henry Humdinger,' Botty Smugpantz was telling his brother. 'His head was chopped off – it took six blows of the axe to do it – enough to make him haunt people, don't you think?'

I nodded. The Adviser nodded.

'Or it might be Lady Laurabelle. She hurled herself out of the window.'

The Adviser shivered. I shivered.

'Or poor little Lord Corduroy; he was only six years old when his uncle murdered him – he stabbed him with a ten-foot sword.'

'The ghost in the Palace sounds like it's being murdered all right!' Adviser Smugpantz said.

'Hope it's the little chap,' Botty Smugpantz said. 'I wouldn't mind dealing with a *small* ghost.'

'I'd rather we didn't have to deal with any ghosts.'

The Adviser scratched his head. I scratched my ear.

Botty Smugpantz suddenly spotted me.

'Go away, fleabag!'

'Are you talking to me?' cried the Adviser.

'No! The dog!' yelled Botty Smugpantz. 'Were you listening, Pong? Did you hear what I said? Not that size matters or anything,' he went on. 'Not that I'm frightened or anything

and not that it has anything to do with you!
Mongrel!'

I wasn't going to hang around to be called
names. I went.

The next wizard I came across was Wizard
Whitelock. He had fallen asleep on the sofa.
No need to worry about him, then.

Wizard Winston was lounging in the garden on a sunbed.

'What sort of wizardry do you do?' I asked him. 'Is it modern magic, or the old-fashioned sort?'

Winston stroked my left ear in an off-hand way. He was concentrating on drinking a pink ice-cream soda through a curly straw.

'To tell you the truth, Pong, I don't do much, really,' Winston said. He lay back and adjusted his sunglasses. 'I found this old gown in a green bin, saw the proclamation and thought I'd come along for fun.'

I stuck my nose up against the gown and sniffed. Of course! It was Wizard Wazp's gown that I'd put out for recycling. And it had recycled.

'Aren't you a wizard or magician of any sort?'

Winston shook his head.

'But you'll have to do some wizardry if you want to stay,' I said.

'Maybe. Maybe I won't want to stay. Anyway, something tells me you're a wizard sort of dog yourself. You'll catch the ghost!'

'Nice of you to say, but I could do with some help.'

'Naturally I'll help, Pong.' He patted my head. 'If it's not too scary, too rough, too exhausting, too difficult or too time-consuming,' Winston said. 'There's not much to do around here is there? Say, how about a game of ping pong, Pong? Do you like ping pong, Pong?'

'Certainly!' I wagged my tail.

'Fab! You're on!'

We had a great game but Winston tired easily and retired for a snooze.

I wandered over to the old rose garden to see how the new lake was coming along. I was worried: I had to catch the Palace ghost, but without a good spell and without a proper wizard, how was I going to do it?

The workmen had gone home. The place was a mess.

I was going to pee on the newly turned earth, but I've had some bad moments with rose bushes, so I was dithering. Then I spotted something:

A BONE!

Saliva dripped. My tail went on automatic wag. *Bone*. Yum yum. Bone. It's the marrow, you know, that's so scrumptious; it takes a long, long time to get it out, you have to get your tongue right inside it and squelch about and suck.

The bone wasn't very big, but it could give me hours of fun if I didn't get carried away and crunch up the whole thing in one bite. I eased it out of the soil and carried it up to the Spell Chamber to enjoy later.

I had another go at TESCO, but it was 'Closed for Refurbishment'.

Chapter 7

Ghost Hunters

That night we prepared to catch the ghost.

Wizard 'Botty' Smugpantz was hiding in a wardrobe outside the King's bedroom with the Adviser.

Wizard Whitelock was dozing on a chair beside the wardrobe.

Wizard Winston and I were in an empty bedroom nearby. I don't know how Winston got himself a bed for the night, but he was the sort of chap that would get a bed if there was one to get.

We played 'Snap' and 'Cheat', which Winston was extremely good at. We told each other

riddles and jokes until midnight and I could see
I'd have to think of something more exciting
soon, as Winston was getting sleepy.

'Well,' Winston yawned.
'I don't think—'

A terrible *Yeowl!* split
the quiet night air.

YEOWL!

ZzZz

KING
ASLEEP
DO NOT

'Good garden rhubarb!' Winston cried, throwing his cards up in the air. 'What was that?'

Another blood-curdling scream flooded the building followed by a ghastly screech.

'It's the ghost!' I said. 'Come on!'

'You have to be joking.' Winston pulled the sheets over his head. 'That sounds horrible. I'm staying here. I thought the King had maybe imagined this spook, but that sounds real – really scary!'

'Couldn't you just—' I said.

'No way!' Winston said. 'Can't be done, Pong. I'm terrified! 'There was nothing else for it, I stepped out into the corridor alone.

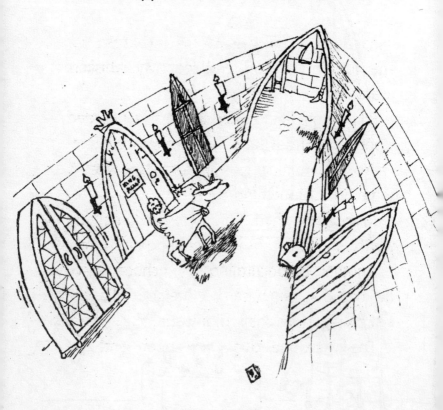

Moonlight gleamed in through the tall windows. Candles flickered in brackets along the walls. Shadows danced.

YEOWL! WAAAH!

Each and every hair on my back rose up. The fur on my ears crackled. My whiskers twanged.

Forcing my tail to stand up perkily, I tiptoed along the corridor, watching for any movement. There was nothing to see, but I could sense something. Something *not alive*.

My nose twitched. Now there was something whiffy, something fishy, something not right.

Another bloodcurdling cry echoed down the corridor, but Wizard Whitelock, who was fast asleep in his chair, didn't stir.

The wardrobe door flew open and the

Adviser and Botty Smugpantz popped out like corks from a bottle of fizz. I slunk back in the shadows behind a chest.

'I heard that! Where is it?' Botty roared. 'I'll catch it! I'll get it! Watch out, bro – I'll use my *Light up the Darkest Dark* spell to see it!'

He whispered some magic words and circled his wand around. The tip of the wand gleamed brightly and the whole passageway was illuminated.

It was empty.

'Odd!' Wizard Botty whacked the wand against his thigh. 'Not working. There's nothing there!'

'Try something else,' the Adviser suggested.

'Very well. I'll try the *Cobweb Cascade*.'

Wizard Botty muttered more magic words and waved his wand again. A gossamer thin veil appeared, hovering in the air like a fine, green cobweb. The web floated backwards and forwards as if it was searching for something.

'It drops onto invisible human forms and makes them visible,' Botty explained. But the web was unable to find a human form to drop onto and after a few minutes it dissolved.

'No *human form*?' Botty's voice trembled. 'What sort of a ghost is it?'

We hadn't heard a sausage for a full five minutes, but all of a sudden an awful shriek and howl sounded right beside us. I jumped. The two Smugpantz actually rose off the ground and into the air:

53

Their gowns swirled. Their black hair stuck out like black rods.

Whah! They thudded back onto the stone floor.

'Help!' the Adviser cried.

'You're the Adviser! Advise us what to do!' Botty shrieked.

'Run for it!' the Adviser cried.

They dashed to the nearest chamber and slammed and bolted the door shut behind them.

I, however, being of stronger mettle, stood my ground. Pedigree Shippo Pom-Poms do not run away from anything.

I pricked up my ears; flicked them round, like radar panels to catch the smallest sound . . . And yes! Ah ha! There! The softest pad, pad of paws! The smallest sigh, like a fine silk cloth passing through a wedding ring! The tiniest ssshhhhh of rippling fur!

I spun round in time to see the creature pass through a band of moonlight. Two yellow eyes turned towards me and glinted golden in the light.

CAT! CAT! CAT!

My brain fizzed.

I forgot I was on an important mission. I only knew I was a DOG and that was a CAT. My legs were on the go, and there was nothing I could do to stop them.

I sped full tilt down the corridor towards the cat, barking and howling. My jaws were snapping like a croc. Saliva sprayed the walls.

Woof woof! Yeroow!

My tail spun.

I chased the cat down the corridor; suits of armour flashed by, grandfather clocks, cobwebbed cupboards, a line of stern portraits, closed doors, curtained windows . . . I skidded round a bend – the corridor came to a dead end. There was nowhere for the cat to go. I had it cornered.

Woof! Woof! Yeroow!

I put on the brakes. Got it!

But no!

To my utter amazement, without even a glance in my direction, the cat leaped straight at the thick stone wall.

And disappeared.

What sort of a cat could do that?

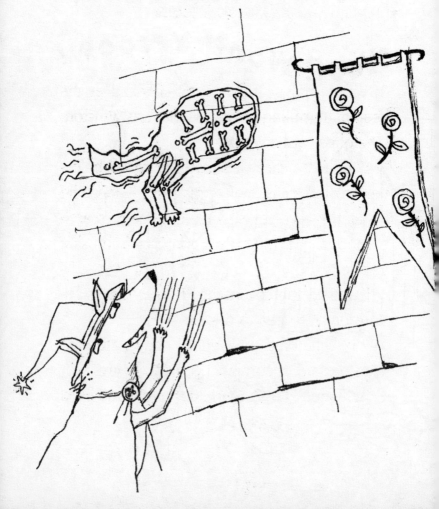

Chapter 8

A Wizard Plan

'It was a *ghost* cat, Winston!' I yelled at the heap of trembling bedcovers that was Winston. 'The ghost was a cat!'

Winston's face appeared from below the covers. His hair was wild and the whites of his eyes shone. 'I'm really scared of ghosts,' he mumbled, looking from side to side.

I yanked the covers further off. 'Come on, Winston! We need to catch it!'

'I've changed my mind about staying,' Winston said, gloomily. 'I can't stay here.'

'Why not?' I asked him. 'I thought you liked

the castle comforts and you like ping pong, don't you?'

'Sure, but I don't like ghosts.'

'Even pussy-cat ghosts?'

'Not even kitten-cat ghosts!' he shivered. 'Oooer, it was awful.'

'Maybe you'll feel better in the morning,' I suggested.

'Maybe I'll feel worse!'

There was nothing I could say or do to change his mind so we settled down together in the bed. I formulated a clever plan. Winston had nightmares and tossed about as if he were fighting demons.

He didn't feel better in the morning.

'Definitely leaving,' he said, handing me the old wizard gown. 'Hope you win the competition, Pong, you're a wizard dog!' He patted me. 'Good luck!' And he was gone.

I was on my own again, but during the night I had made a plan.

I scampered off to the Palace Library and dragged out the Royal Photograph Albums.

There was a most particular photo I needed. Next I sent a message to the King to come and meet me at the rose garden.

Ha ha! My clever plan would show them how brilliant I was!

They'd have to make me the next Royal Wizard!

The King, bless him, brought along the Adviser, Botty Smugpantz and Wizard Whitelock to the old rose garden too.

We gathered beside the mess of stones and earth and spades and stared at the giant hole that was to be the lake.

'Where's that Winston chap?' the Adviser asked.

'He's decided to move on,' I told him.

'You mean he knew he'd lose!' Botty cried. 'Ha! Good riddance to bad rubbish!'

The King waved at the garden. 'It's going to be a jolly fine lake, what?' he said.

I put the photo down carefully on the grass. 'Yes,' I said. 'It is. But do you remember what was here before?'

'A rose garden.' A faraway look came into the King's eyes. 'The Queen loved roses. The rose garden was her favourite, favourite spot.' He dabbed his eyes with a hanky.

'Exactly,' I said. 'Watch!'

I dived into the freshly turned soil and began digging.

Perhaps it would have been better if I'd explained first, because Botty and Ambrose Smugpantz immediately began making rude comments:

'Dogs! Dirty things. You just can't cure them of their bad habits, can you?'

'Dogs must be banned from the Royal Garden,' Adviser Smugpantz said. 'I will change the laws. I shall write a decree.'

'Pong is making a bit of a mess,' the King agreed.

'He's digging something up,' Botty said. 'Look! Bones!'

At this point I should definitely have spoken, but when you get earth between your toes and the scent of bones in your nostrils, the smell of wet earth . . .

'I told you,' the Adviser said. 'Dogs are brainless. Just smelly four-legged creatures invented to chase cats.'

Botty, meanwhile, picked up the photograph that I had taken out of the Royal Album and left on the grass.

'What's this?' Botty said. 'A cat?'

I stopped digging. Whoops! I shouldn't have left the photo unguarded. I yelped, 'Woof!'

'See how excited the dog gets at the mention of a cat?' said the Adviser. 'Tut tut tut!'

'Who's that ugly old trout holding that scabby fat cat?' Botty went on. 'What a hideous moggy!'

The Adviser turned away and stared into the distance as if he had heard nothing, was not with us, and was in some way, highly superior to everything and everyone. He was as still as a statue.

The King went perfectly bright red and exploded.

'That's my Queen!' he shouted. 'My dear Queen! How dare you!'

'I didn't – I wouldn't – I thought . . .' stammered Botty.

'No one must speak ill of my wife! You're disqualified!' the King said. 'Go!'

'No! No! Brother, help me!' Wizard Botty dropped to his knees in front of the Adviser, but the Adviser looked the other way. 'Please?' No answer. 'Please, Amb**rose!**'

'A *rose*?' Old Wizard Whitelock perked up suddenly. 'Yes, lovely roses, lovely. Smell good too. I remember that stinky old cat Tabbykins was buried here, wasn't it? Cat smelt like it had been set on fire then left out in the rain, ha, ha!'

'And you're disqualified too!' the King shouted. 'Leave our Palace immediately, both of you!'

As you can imagine, I wagged my tail like mad. Good old King, not such a nitwit after all.

'Didn't I win, then?' said Wizard Whitelock. 'Never even saw the ghost. Never mind. I'll be home in time for a nap.'

'Be quiet, you silly old fool!' the Adviser shouted. 'And go!'

Wizard Botty took Wizard Whitelock's arm and hurried him away as fast as the old wizard's legs would go.

Chapter 9

The Small Print

'My Queen was such a fine darling wife!' the King said, gazing at the photo. 'And dear old Tabbykins – how she loved that cat!' He dabbed at his eyes again. 'Tabbykins was buried beneath the Queen's favourite rose in her rose garden.'

'Was he?' the Adviser asked.

'Yes!' I jumped in quickly. 'That's why I found the photo and brought you here,' I said. 'When the gardeners disturbed the bones, the cat's ghost was annoyed – and came and haunted you.'

'What? Do you mean the ghost is a *cat*?' the King said.

'I do,' I said. 'Here we are, here are his bones.' And I dropped the bones at his feet.

'Tabbykins!' the King cried. 'Well done, Po—'

But before he could get any further, the Adviser, slimy sneak that he is, interrupted.

'Better not let Pong play with these,' he said, picking the bones up. 'I think we should collect them up and lay them to rest again under another rose bush, don't you?'

'But that was my idea!' I said. 'That's a bit *rough*!'

'Barking again. Tut, tut, hush, Pong,' the Adviser said. 'Dogs don't have ideas, do they? Just fleas.'

The King kissed the photo of his wife.

'Well done, Adviser! Where would I be without you!'

'You'd still be being haunted,' I reminded him. 'Listen, please. I brought that photo. I solved the mystery of the ghost. I should be the Royal Wizard.'

'Well you have got a point, Pong,' the King said. 'Come and see me later. Six o'clock in the Royal Snug.'

Joy of joys! I wagged my tail wildly. At last I was going to get rewarded!

I could hardly wait for six o'clock to come. I would be the first canine wizard in Palace history!

I trotted in to see the King at the appointed time, tail held high, black nose in the air.

I was very unhappy to see the rotten old Adviser was standing next to the King. He was holding a long document and he looked *smug*.

'Pong, I'm very grateful to you for ridding the Palace of that ghost,' the King said, 'but I'm afraid I cannot make you Royal Wizard. The Adviser has pointed out something to me in the small print here, in the job description for Royal Wizard—'

'Yes?'

'To be Royal Wizard you need to speak a foreign language,' the King said.

'And you can't, can you, Pong?' said the Adviser bending low and grinning at me.

He was cheating again. The scoundrel was cheating!

'You can't, can you? *Comprends? Capisci?*'

Well, I couldn't understand those foreign
languages, but there was one . . .

I stared at him, frankly, eyeball to eyeball.
'*Miaow*,' I said.